This book belongs to:

_____

Published by Ladybird Books Ltd
A Penguin Company

Penguin Books Ltd., 80 Strand, London WC2R 0RL, UK
Penguin Books Australia Ltd., Camberwell, Victoria, Australia
Penguin Books (NZ) Ltd., Private Bag 102902, NSMC, Auckland, New Zealand

This book is based on the TV episode "A Cloudy Day in Sunny Patch", written by
Steven Sullivan, from the animated TV series *Miss Spider's Sunny Patch Friends* on
Nick Jr, a Nelvana Limited/Absolute Pictures Limited co-production in association with
Callaway Arts & Entertainment, based on the Miss Spider books by David Kirk.

First published by Ladybird Books 2005
3 5 7 9 10 8 6 4 2

ISBN-13: 978-1-84422-752-5
ISBN-10: 1-84422-752-9

Printed in Italy

Miss Spider's

SUNNY PATCH FRIENDS

A Cloudy Day
in Sunny Patch

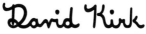

David Kirk

It was almost Shimmer's eighth hatchday, and she was so excited – her family was throwing her first hatchday party ever!

"Tell me, Shimmer, what kind of party do you want?" asked Miss Spider.

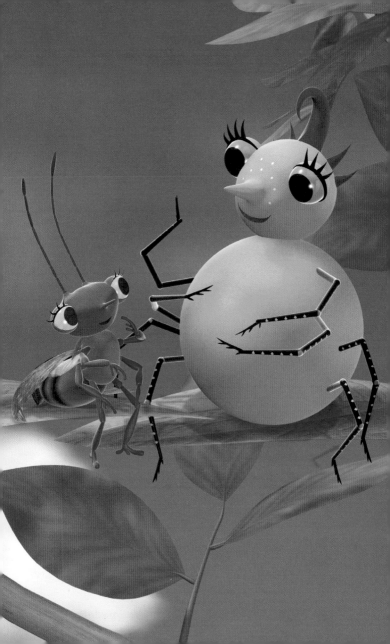

"That's easy!" laughed Shimmer. "I want to have my party at the Taddy Puddle.

"I want ribbons and flowers and funny hats. I want a great big fruitcake with strawberry lice cream. Then I want to go swimming and play beach buggy-ball!"

Miss Spider and her children
planned the party.

"Dragon, Pansy and I can set
up the games!" Squirt said.

"We'll make a web banner with
a big number eight!" Snowdrop
and Wiggle exclaimed.

"I'll help bake
the cake!"
said
Bounce.

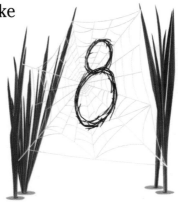

Finally, it was Shimmer's hatchday. Everybuggy was busy getting ready when a rain cloud filled the sky.

Miss Spider looked up and
sighed, "Oh no."

Shimmer heard thunder in the distance.

"Is that what I think it is?" she asked.

Rain poured down.

The little bugs ran inside.

Shimmer was miserable.

"I'm sorry, honey," said Miss Spider. "Sometimes nature makes us change our plans."

"We can still have fun," said Squirt. "Let's play hide-and-seek!"

"I'm it! I'm it! I'm it!" shouted Bounce, closing his eyes and turning his back.
"I'll count!"

"But there's no place to hide!"
Shimmer whined. "This isn't the
hatchday party I wanted at all."

"I know a game you'd love to play!" shouted Dragon. "Beach buggy-ball!"

He took a long swing and smacked the ball with all his might . . .

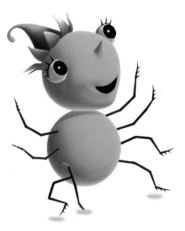

. . . right into the hatchday cake.

Shimmer's eyes filled with tears.

She cried harder and harder.

Her cries turned to sobs.

Her sobs turned into a wail.

But then her wail turned into a
chuckle, her chuckle turned to
a giggle, and then finally a great
big laugh.

"What's so funny, honey?"
asked Miss Spider.

"What's funny?" Shimmer
exclaimed. "Just look at us!"

"When your family loves you,"
Shimmer smiled, "I guess you
can have fun doing anything!"

Soon, the rain stopped. The
party moved back to the Taddy
Puddle, where they all danced
and played into the night.